What is Indiana
in Sept

Indy's pal Remy enlists in the Belgian army to fight the Germans and is sent to France. Indy goes with him . . . And not just for the ride!

Come along with Indy to the battlegrounds of World War I, where his courage and daring are tested as never before! Meet the famous generals who call the shots. And the ordinary soldiers who fire them.

Catch the whole story of Young Indy's travels on the amazing fact-and-fiction television series *The Young Indiana Jones Chronicles!*

THE YOUNG INDIANA JONES CHRONICLES
(novels based on the television series)

YOUNG INDIANA JONES BOOKS
(original novels)

Young Indiana Jones and the . . .

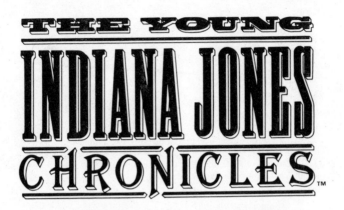

THE YOUNG INDIANA JONES CHRONICLES™

Field of Death

Adapted by Les Martin

Based on the teleplay "Verdun, September 1916"
by Jonathan Hensleigh

Story by George Lucas

Directed by Rene Manzor

With photographs from the television show

RANDOM HOUSE 🏠 NEW YORK

This is a work of fiction. While Young Indiana Jones is portrayed as taking part in historical events and meeting real figures from history, many of the characters in the story as well as the situations and scenes have been invented. In addition, where real historical figures and events are described, in some cases the chronology and historical facts have been altered for dramatic effect.

PHOTO CREDITS: Cover photograph by Jaromir Komarek, © 1991 by Lucasfilm Ltd. Interior photographs by Jaromir Komarek, © 1992 by Lucasfilm Ltd. Map by Alfred Giuliani.

Library of Congress Cataloging-in-Publication Data
Martin, Les.
Field of death / adapted by Les Martin ; teleplay by Jonathan Hensleigh ; story by George Lucas ; directed by Rene Manzor.
p. cm.—(The Young Indiana Jones chronicles ; TV-2)
"Based on the television episode Verdun, September 1916, with photographs from the show."
Includes bibliographical references.
Summary: As a courier for the French army at the Battle of Verdun, young Indiana Jones finds himself battling the French generals who persist in ordering suicidal assaults against the German troops.
ISBN 0-679-82775-7 (pbk.)
1. Verdun, Battle of, 1916—Juvenile fiction. 2. World War, 1914–1918—Campaigns—France—Juvenile fiction. [1. Verdun, Battle of, 1916—Fiction. 2. World War, 1914–1918—Campaigns—France—Fiction. 3. Adventure and adventurers—Fiction.] I. Hensleigh, Jonathan. II. Lucas, George. III. Manzor, Rene. IV. Title. V. Series.
PZ7.M36353Fi 1992 [Fic]—dc20 91-53164

Manufactured in the United States of America 10 9 8 7 6 5 4 3 2

TM & © 1992 Lucasfilm Ltd. (LFL). All rights reserved.

Field of Death

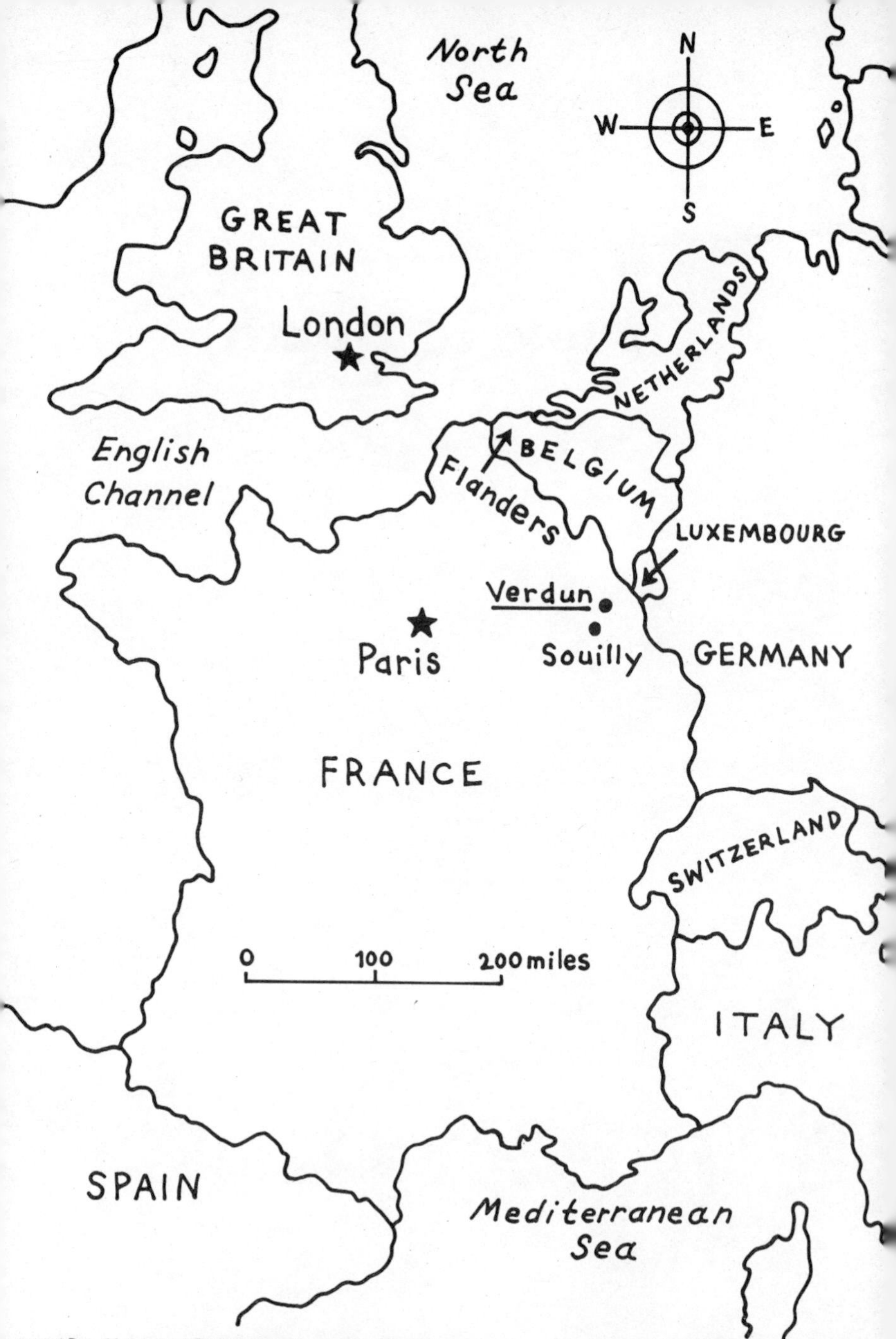

INDY'S TERRITORY IN "VERDUN, SEPTEMBER 1916"

Chapter 1

"Soldier! Let's see your papers!"

The order came from behind young Indiana Jones. It was in French, but Indy had no trouble understanding it. Though he was only seventeen, his French was very good. His accent was nearly perfect. He spoke German and a few other languages as well. That was one thing he had to give his dad, Professor Henry Jones, credit for. The professor had encouraged Indy to master as many languages as he could. Languages were tools Indy would need to follow in his dad's footsteps as a scholar.

Right now, though, Indy had strayed far from his dad's footsteps. And far from home. He was wearing a Belgian army uniform. And he was in Paris, the capital city of France.

Indy turned to find himself facing a big, bearded man wearing the light-blue uniform of the French army. On the man's head was the French infantry helmet, with its ridge across the center from back to front. On his sleeves were sergeant's stripes.

Indy knew why the sergeant had singled him out. Indy's Belgian uniform was brown. It stood out from the sea of blue uniforms around him. They filled the Gare de l'Est, the vast railway station where all trains to and from the east of France came and went. One train after another, arriving and departing in an endless shuttle.

All were troop trains, and all of them were packed. The Gare de l'Est was the jumping-off point for Verdun, and the end of the line for those returning from it.

Once upon a time, two long years ago, Verdun had been nothing more than the name of an old and honored French city. Now, however, it had another meaning for all of France. Verdun was now the name of one of the most savage battles of the most savage war the world had ever known—the war the world had come to call the Great War.

The war had broken out in August 1914. The politicians said it would be short and sweet. No one said that now. No one knew when it would end, or how.

Indy handed the sergeant his papers.

"Corporal Henri Défense," the sergeant read aloud. "Army of Belgium. Assigned as courier to General Staff Headquarters in Souilly." He peered closely at Indy. "You seem a bit young to be a soldier, my boy."

Indy made his voice as deep as he could. "I'm twenty, Sergeant. All my family look young. My father, for instance, does not look a day over thirty-five."

"And a corporal, too," the sergeant persisted.

"I was given my second stripe after a battle in Flanders," Indy said. "Everyone in my company was promoted—everyone who survived. There wasn't much of a Belgian army left after that. And with our country in the hands of the Germans, we were merged into the army of France."

"Yes, Flanders was a bad business," the sergeant agreed. "But believe me, it was a picnic compared to what you're going to." He handed Indy back his papers. "Still, you're to be assigned to the General Staff. They always stay a safe distance behind the front, count on that. Of course, as a courier, you will have to go to the front with messages. But just quickly, in and out. Not like those poor devils stuck in the front-line trenches."

A chill ran through Indy as he thought of one of those "poor devils." His pal, Remy Baudouin. Remy hadn't been as lucky as Indy. After Flanders, Remy had been assigned to the French infantry. He and Indy had been split up. Since then, Indy's only news of Remy had come on a postcard from Verdun. It read: "It was an American general who said that war is hell. He was right."

Indy had met Remy half a year ago in Mexico. Both of them had been caught up by the idealistic promises of revolutionary leader Pancho Villa. They were risking their lives alongside the Villistas when they found out that Belgium was fighting for her life against the invading Germans. Remy had headed back to Europe to help defend his native land. Indy had come along for more than the boat ride. His friend Ned Lawrence had said the war against Germany was a war that "must be won." That was enough for Indy. Besides, he wanted to be where the action was.

He got there quick and easy. In London Indy and Remy found the shabby Belgian recruiting office. Thinking he needed to be Belgian, Indy made a quick decision. He changed his birth date and borrowed a new last name from the no smoking sign, *Défense de fumer.* He became Henri Défense! The recruiter accepted his false name without question. Indy found out why in the watery trenches of Flanders. Belgium desperately needed anyone she could get who could pull a trigger. The war had a ravenous appetite for fighting men. Division after division had been chewed up.

A sharp train whistle cut through the hubbub of the station. A locomotive came grinding to a halt. The concrete train platforms of the station were in the open air, and the smoke from the locomotive merged with the gray of the Paris sky. A light rain was falling. Through the drizzle Indy could see a line of train cars stretching out of sight.

"That's your train," the sergeant told Indy. "You board as soon as they unload it. Good luck,

Corporal." The sergeant smiled grimly. "You can wish me the same thing. I'm taking the same train you are."

Indy stood beside the sergeant and watched the train empty.

Soldiers poured from the first cars. Their steps were eager.

"They're coming home on leave," the sergeant told Indy. "Front-line troops are given leaves regularly—or else they'd crack."

"They look in pretty good shape," Indy remarked.

"Before they get on the train to Paris, they have to stop at a troop center behind the lines," the sergeant said. "First, of course, they have to be deloused. Next they get any cases of trench foot taken care of. Those sores on the feet can be pretty painful. Then they get clean uniforms, haircuts, shaves. They have to look good for the people back home. Or else people might not be so eager to support the war."

"And the soldiers themselves?" Indy asked. "What do they think about the war?"

The sergeant shrugged. His mouth was a tight, silent line.

Indy looked at the faces of the soldiers

streaming past, heading for the exits. He saw vacant expressions and glazed eyes. He had once seen a boxer staggering around the ring after taking a vicious left hook. These faces reminded him of that guy, out on his feet.

After the first wave of soldiers came another, larger wave—the walking wounded.

They wore splints and bandages; they limped or swung themselves along on crutches. Some were leading others, whose eyes were covered with bandages. Outside the train station Indy had seen rows of army buses and troop trucks. Now he knew what they were for, and where they would go: to hospitals well out of public view.

Next came the biggest wave of all, the men lying silent or groaning on stretchers. They seemed to pass by forever.

"They're the ones in good shape," the sergeant commented. "They're the ones who could survive the train trip. At least, the doctors hoped so."

Indy gulped. He thought he had seen the worst that war could do, in Flanders. But that did not compare to this.

"There must have been a flare-up in the

fighting," he said.

The sergeant gave a mirthless laugh. Then he spat. "Not at all, my boy. This is just an ordinary day. You don't want to have to see what the day of a big attack by us or the Germans will bring." He sighed and for a brief moment put a gentle hand on Indy's shoulder. "But I'm afraid you will. There'll be no escaping it when you go to Verdun."

Chapter 2

In the Gare de l'Est, Indy had his first view of the battle of Verdun. He could see the horrors that the men leaving the train must have faced. But there was another way to look at the battle. The way that generals did. On a map.

In the case of Verdun, the map of the battle zone lay on a gleaming oak table in an elegant ballroom in a magnificent chateau in Souilly, over ten miles from Verdun. The chateau was headquarters for the French General Staff. Here they pushed pins around on the map to chart the course of the fighting.

On the map, the battle seemed simple. It centered on a dot that marked the city of Verdun itself. A few inches away was a line that marked the French trenches. Inches from that was the line that marked the German trenches. And just behind that was a dot that marked the stronghold of Fort Douaumont.

At one time Douaumont was the strongest of French fortresses. But in February 1916, a handful of Germans captured it in a surprise attack. Now their finest troops held this strongpoint commanding the heights overlooking Verdun.

"Douaumont. It's the key to victory at Verdun," said General Robert Nivelle. He was a picture of what a general should look like, distinguished, confident, and commanding. And he had no doubt of what a general's job should be. "We must attack and take Douaumont as soon as possible."

He extended a long, elegant finger to touch the map. His well-manicured fingernail moved three inches on the map to capture Douaumont. It was as simple as that.

Standing beside him, his aide, General Charles Mangin, nodded. His mustached mouth smiled in admiration. "Thank God you are now in command of the Second Army. How we have needed a commander willing to attack."

"Thank you, Charles," General Nivelle said. "Perhaps now we can fight this war properly."

"Spoken like a true leader," said Mangin, still fawning. He went on to say exactly what he knew Nivelle wanted to hear, for Nivelle had said it often enough himself. "General Petain did a good enough job keeping the Germans from breaking through to Verdun after they took Douaumont. But the time for his kind of war is over. No more cowardly hiding in trenches. Now we must go over the top and fight like men in the open. Marshal Joffre knows that. That is why he kicked Petain upstairs to command the whole sector. He wanted to put a man like you in charge of the real fighting."

"Petain." Nivelle's mouth curled in contempt. "Always worrying about blood. As if blood were not part of war. The loss of Douaumont is a stain on French honor. Only French blood can wash it out."

"Allow me," said Mangin, and poured both

Nivelle and himself a glass of champagne. "Let us toast our success."

Nivelle raised his glass. "Yes, fighting in trenches is for animals. One great push and Douaumont will collapse like a house of cards. Soon we will toast victory—with German wine."

Mangin was about to refill their glasses when the door opened. Mangin put down the bottle as a young major named Marat stepped in. Behind him was General Philippe Petain.

General Petain had spent most of his sixty years in the French army. He was a soldier from the soles of his polished boots to the top of his bald head. His eyes were a soldier's eyes. They had seen everything, and trusted nothing they could not see for themselves. They were weary and wary eyes.

"Greetings, General Petain!" Nivelle said, as Mangin poured a welcoming glass of champagne.

Petain ignored it. "Charles. Robert. You're cheerful today."

"We are at war," Nivelle declared. "War raises a soldier's spirit."

"Does it?" Petain curtly replied.

"What would give *you* happiness, Philippe?"

asked Mangin, sipping the champagne he had poured for Petain.

Petain was standing by one of the ballroom's floor-to-ceiling windows. He looked out at the peaceful forest surrounding the chateau.

"The safe return of our men," he said, as if speaking to himself. "And an end to this madness." With an effort of will, he turned away from the lush and gentle scene outside. He faced Nivelle and Mangin. "Why don't you show me your plans?"

"We're waiting for Marshal Joffre," Nivelle said, uneasily.

"I am your sector commander," Petain said, with iron in his voice. "What is the status of the operations?"

Nivelle and Mangin exchanged helpless glances. They went with Petain to the large cloth map, which had been spread out on a billiard table.

"We are going to retake Fort Douaumont. We attack here—directly at the north side of it," said Nivelle. He picked up a cue stick and pointed to the spot with an elegant gesture.

"Artillery preparation?" Petain demanded.

"It will be adequate," Mangin said.

"What is the purpose of the new attack?" Petain went on. "We attacked the north side three weeks ago."

"Purpose?" said Nivelle, puzzled.

"The men will be rushing entrenched machine guns and artillery," said Petain. "Uphill. One would hope that you have a purpose in mind."

There was dead silence as Nivelle evaded Petain's demanding gaze.

Suddenly the door was opened again.

Major Marat entered and saluted. "Sirs. Marshal Joffre."

Marshal Joffre wore the weight of many good meals like a medal. His uniform bulged, and one could almost scent rich sauces and fine wines in his walrus mustache. His answer to the sharp salutes that greeted him was a sloppy wave of his hand toward his forehead. He did not try to look much like a soldier. He did not have to. He and the generals standing before him knew that he was commander of the army of France, and his word was law.

"At ease, gentlemen," the marshal said. He flashed the warm smile that charmed politicians, reporters, and the public. His eyes had the cold calculation that made him a master player at the ruthless chess game of war. "I haven't much time. I'm expected at the ballet. The war minister and his wife will be there. The reason I'm here is to discuss the problem with your communication network."

"Marshal Joffre—" Nivelle began.

Joffre cut him short. "Don't protest, Robert. Your telephone lines have been destroyed by German shells, and the Germans have spies among your couriers."

"I have dealt with the problem, Marshal," Nivelle said. "New couriers—Belgians."

"Belgians." Joffre grimaced. "An inferior lot. Can you depend on them? Dependable communications are vital to the war effort—and to your career, Robert."

"Why don't we see what they can do?" Nivelle said, and walked to the map.

Joffre's eyes lit up. "You have an operation in mind?"

"Yes, as a matter of fact," said Nivelle. He was speaking to Joffre, but his gloating gaze was on Petain.

Joffre looked at the spot on the map that Nivelle pointed to. "Fort Douaumont?" he said. "Wonderful. When?"

"Right now," Nivelle said.

Joffre rubbed his hands together. "I want the results as soon as possible. It is time I had some good news to give the press."

Joffre turned to leave. But he was stopped by Petain's indignant voice.

"Wait a moment."

Joffre looked at Petain, who had drawn himself up to his full, commanding height.

"Yes, General?" Joffre inquired.

"You can't authorize another attack from that position," Petain protested.

"I just did," Joffre replied.

"An attack on Douaumont? Just like that?" Petain said in a pained voice. "What about the strength of the enemy position? How many men do the Germans have? How many guns? What about the weather? Must the senior staff be reminded that . . ." He paused, before his anger got the better of him.

"That what, General?" Nivelle asked icily.

"Spit it out, Philippe," Joffre ordered.

"That an attack is easy to order from the comfort of this room," Petain said in a cutting tone. "It is quite another thing for the men in the trenches to carry out."

"What is that supposed to mean?" Nivelle demanded. "Are you suggesting that our soldiers are not brave? Are they not the finest fighting men on earth?"

"Yes, perhaps you should explain further," Joffre said. His voice, however, did not sound as though he was very interested in an answer.

"An attack of this magnitude must be planned to the last detail," Petain declared firmly. "This is not a recommendation. I insist on it."

"You *insist*?" Mangin said, sucking in his breath.

"I am the sector commander," Petain said. He turned to Joffre. "I expect your support, Marshal."

Nivelle and Mangin looked at each other, waiting for Joffre's response. Joffre's response was—silence.

Petain's face seemed to turn to stone. He gave a cold salute, wheeled, and left the room, his body rigid with rage.

As soon as he was gone, Nivelle said, "Thank you, Marshal Joffre. I'll start the artillery barrage right away."

Already he was scribbling out orders. When Major Marat entered the room to escort Joffre out, Nivelle handed Marat the orders.

"Dispatch to the front, Major," Nivelle said. "Give it to one of the new Belgian couriers."

19

Before Joffre left, he put his hand on Nivelle's arm. "I chose you to command the fighting because you are not afraid to attack. Succeed at all costs. Don't let me down."

"I promise you, I won't," said Nivelle, as he and Mangin exchanged smiles. He turned to Major Marat. "Make sure the Belgian courier is fast. The fastest we have."

Marat wasted no time in carrying out his orders. As soon as he deposited Joffre in the staff car waiting to speed the marshal to the ballet, the major headed at the quickstep to the courier compound. There he demanded of the sergeant in charge, "Who's the fastest of your Belgians?"

Without hesitation the sergeant pointed to a young soldier playing handball by himself against a wall.

"That new one," the sergeant said, "rides like the wind."

"What's his name?" asked Marat.

"Défense, sir," said the sergeant. "Corporal Henri Défense."

Chapter 3

Indy gave the handball one last hard slam against the wall when he heard the sergeant shout, "Corporal Défense. Come here. On the double."

Indy caught the rebounding ball with one hand, wiped sweat off his forehead with the other, and obeyed.

He gave Major Marat a sharp salute, and received a leather dispatch bag and his orders.

"Get these to Colonel Barc at his battalion

headquarters," Marat snapped. "Fast. As if your life depended on it. A lot of lives do."

It took Indy less than two minutes to hop on his motorcycle. He gunned the engine. The bike leaped forward in a shower of gravel.

The French politicians and press called the road to Verdun "la Voie Sacrée," the Sacred Way. It was the lifeline to the front, to be kept open at any cost.

Soldiers had a different name for it.

The Road to Hell.

According to a sign that Indy whizzed past, Verdun was thirteen kilometers away. Eight miles to Hell, thought Indy.

Indy wove through the traffic at breakneck speed. He passed endless trucks carrying supplies, and countless marching soldiers in full field gear. He skidded by repair crews working on the road around the clock to repair damage from German artillery. He saw the landscape whizzing by change from lush countryside to a scene as barren and cratered as the surface of the moon. For months enemy shells had steadily rained down on it, wiping away all greenery.

Indy bounced through the narrow cobbled

streets of Verdun itself. The great cathedral was still standing. But the buildings all around were in ruins. Verdun was a perfect target for German guns.

Beyond the town he passed a line of entrenched French artillery. He saw mountains of used shell casings. And other mountains of shells were being unloaded from trucks by sweating soldiers, naked to the waist. Like the road repair, this, too, went on around the clock. There was no time off from the war at Verdun.

Colonel Barc was headquartered in the reserve trenches. Beyond them, in the direction of the enemy, was a line of support trenches. After that came the front-line trenches. Then barbed wire. Then no-man's-land. Then German barbed wire. Then German trenches. And finally, on high ground, manned by crack German troops and bristling with guns, Fort Douaumont commanded the battlefield.

Indy parked his bike in a large underground shed that served as a motor pool. He entered the trench and asked directions. A grizzled soldier pointed down the trench, and Indy broke into a run. After two years of war, trench building had become a fine art. This trench ran the length of the front. It was deep enough so that the men could safely stand upright, and wide enough to have handcar rails down its center. It had heavily buttressed bunkers to house men and supplies.

Colonel Barc was on the telephone when Indy entered the command bunker. The colonel was tall and lean. His uniform jacket was unbuttoned. His face had a two-day stubble of beard. He would have looked out of place leading a parade—but he looked just right to lead men in battle. Right now his eyes blazed with fury.

"My men need *boots*, Major," he shouted. "Not in two weeks. Not in a week. Not in two days. But *now. My men need new boots*." Barc listened a moment, then slammed down the receiver. "Maybe if the idiots came here and actually *saw* the condition of this rat hole—" The colonel saw Indy. "Who are you?"

"Corporal Henri Défense, sir," Indy said, standing at attention and saluting.

"Disregard my last comment," Barc said.

"What last comment, sir?" Indy said, still at attention, but barely hiding a grin.

Barc smiled. "At ease, Corporal. What's your business?"

Indy extended the dispatch pouch. "From Second Army Command, sir."

Barc yanked the pouch from Indy's hand, ripped it open, and read the orders. His gaunt face paled.

Under his breath he muttered. "No, no, no. This has to be a joke." He looked at his watch. "A bad joke." He went to the phone and frantically cranked it. Then he slammed it down. "The line to Sector Four trenches is down—as usual. Corporal, are you a fast runner?"

"Yes, sir," Indy said.

At that moment, the artillery began booming. Shells exploded in the distance—in the direction of the German lines.

"What's happening, sir?" Indy asked.

"The geniuses in command want an attack on Fort Douaumont," Barc said. "Now, listen to me, Corporal. Our men must begin the attack as soon as our artillery stops, before the Germans have time to recover. Otherwise our troops will be slaughtered. Understand?"

"Y-y-yes," Indy said. His throat felt suddenly dry.

Barc scribbled out orders. "Get this to Lieutenant Gaston in the front lines." He handed the orders to Indy. Indy took a deep breath. Then he was off and running.

His lungs were burning as he raced through the communication trench that led from the reserve trench to the support trench. His mouth tasted of old pennies as he headed from the support trench to the front-line trench. The Germans were answering with their own shell fire now. Dust filled the air in the trenches. Indy dodged around sandbags that had collapsed inward. He raced past machine gunners and mortar teams, all at their weapons. He tore around a bend in the trench and ran right into three soldiers playing cards.

They looked at Indy and a bleak expression passed over their faces.

"A message runner," said one.

"I told you. This one's for us," said another.

Grimly they picked up their rifles.

Meanwhile Indy had torn around another corner, and rammed into a stretcher-bearer waiting for customers.

"Watch where you're going," the man said, picking himself up.

"Where's Lieutenant Gaston?" Indy demanded.

"Right behind you," the man said.

Indy turned to see Gaston in the doorway of his sandbag bunker. There was no way to tell his rank except by his tarnished officer's bars. Otherwise he looked as battered and bone weary as his men.

He read Colonel Barc's scribbled orders.

"I really can't believe this, not again," he groaned. Then his jaw tightened. He put a whistle to his lips and gave a shrill blast.

A call reverberated from man to man—"Stand to!" The trench turned into a hive of activity as soldiers raced to their attack positions. Weapons were double-checked and ladders raised to the trench rim. Now there was nothing to do but wait until the French guns fell silent and the next whistle sent men over the top.

Gaston remembered Indy. "You ran all the way from Colonel Barc?" he asked.

"Yes, sir," Indy said.

"Good job," Gaston said. "You may have saved a few lives at least." He started walking down the trench to check out the troops and give them what encouragement he could. Over his shoulder he said to Indy, "Stay with me. There'll be more work for you to do soon."

The lieutenant saw an intelligence officer looking at the battlefield through a periscope. Gaston borrowed it and gazed at what awaited his men. Slowly he shook his head as he stared.

Indy felt a tapping on his shoulder. He turned to find himself facing the three card-playing soldiers he had run into earlier.

One of them handed Indy a small wooden box. Indy opened it. Inside were photos, a bundle of letters, and a wedding ring.

"My wife's name is Nicole," the soldier said. "She lives in Marseilles. Her address is here. See she gets this."

"Hold on, I can't take—" Indy protested. But the man's pleading look silenced him.

"Okay. Sure. If it turns out to be necessary," Indy said, and the soldier's huge, callused, dirt-blackened hand clasped Indy's hand gratefully.

Then a thought struck Indy. "Say, you don't happen to know a guy called Remy Baudouin, do you? He's a pal of mine from the Belgian army. Last I heard he was serving in this sector."

The man's brows furrowed. "Baudouin? The name sounds familiar. But it's hard to remember. Guys come and go so fast around here."

Then he brightened. "Now I remember. Yeah, he was here. But he's gone now. He was one of the lucky ones."

Indy gave a sigh of relief. "Got transferred out, huh?"

The soldier gave a dry chuckle. "Nobody gets transferred out of the front lines."

"Then how—?" Indy began, already guessing the answer.

"He bought a nice little wound," the man said. "A beautiful piece of metal in the guts. A first-class ticket to a stretcher ride out of here."

"And maybe right to the grave," the second soldier commented.

"No, it wasn't that bad," the first soldier maintained.

"And how do you know?" the second soldier said. "You're a doctor, I suppose."

"I'm better than any doctor in judging wounds," the first soldier said. "I've been in the front lines for four months now. If you last as long, which I doubt, then you can dispute my word."

But the second soldier had lost interest in the argument. He turned his attention to the third soldier, who was on his knees praying.

"That won't do you any good, my friend," the second soldier said. "If he wants you, he'll take you."

"Who? Who will?" asked the soldier on his knees. His body shook with silent sobs.

The second soldier gave a cackle. "Who? You know as well as I. The only one in charge of this war who never forgets us. Monsieur Death."

Chapter 4

Suddenly there was silence. Everyone in the trenches froze for a split second. Then the silence was shattered by two blasts from Lieutenant Gaston's whistle.

The noise of battle began. The voices of officers and sergeants urging their men over the top. Then the roar of the men as they obeyed. Then the chattering German machine guns and exploding German shells. Then the screams of the wounded.

Indy watched the soldiers climb up the ladders and out of sight. Lieutenant Gaston had left the periscope and Indy took his place. What he saw was a scene from hell. Men being cut down by bullets and blown to pieces by shells. A few survivors staggering forward against all odds, but most turning back, some dragging wounded comrades with them, others simply trying to save themselves.

Indy could take it no longer. The least he could do was help some of the wounded get back to the trenches. He turned away from the periscope and looked up. There on the rim of the trench was the soldier who had handed him the box.

The man toppled over and fell back into the trench. His lifeless eyes stared up at Indy. Others were falling now, too, like overripe fruit from trees.

Indy saw one soldier go to help his wounded buddy. But no sooner had the soldier hoisted his friend across his shoulders than a shell hit both of them. In a split second Indy was over the top, on his way to help them. Except he was too late for one of the soldiers. Indy helped the other soldier to the trenches and returned again. And again.

At last, though, it ended. The German guns

died away. The only sounds were the groans of the wounded.

"Lieutenant Gaston wants to see you," a sergeant told Indy. He took a look at Indy's face and added, "Pull yourself together, soldier. The attack is over, not the war. There's still work to do."

Indy went to Gaston's bunker just as Gaston emerged. The lieutenant stared at Indy with dead eyes. Then he handed Indy a document pouch.

"Take this report back to General Staff Headquarters, Corporal," he commanded.

At that moment the intelligence officer arrived.

"Wait a minute," said Gaston to Indy.

"How many?" the lieutenant asked, turning toward the intelligence officer.

"Four hundred and eighty confirmed dead," the man said. "I don't have any figures yet for the wounded and missing. And of course, the death toll is preliminary."

From the battlefield came a moan of agony. "Help me . . . Please . . . Help me . . . Somebody . . . Please."

"That number will go up," said Gaston, as he opened the pouch to scribble in the fresh fig-

33

ures. Then he laid his hand briefly on Indy's shoulder. "Welcome to Verdun, Corporal."

Indy didn't get to see the reaction of General Nivelle to the results of the attack. He got only as far as Major Marat. The major took the dispatch, asked Indy a few quick questions, then told him to get cleaned up and grab a bite to eat in the kitchen. Squaring his shoulders, Marat entered the General Staff dining room with the report.

Nivelle was just beginning dinner with the other generals and younger officers. The table was covered with a damask cloth and set with fine china and silver. Candlelight bounced off the sparkling crystal. A young officer was playing a clavichord. But no one was listening, except, perhaps, for General Petain. Everyone else was laughing at a joke Nivelle had told.

"The casualty report, sir," said Marat, with a brisk salute.

Nivelle paused with a piece of heavily buttered roll halfway to his mouth. "Which one?" he asked.

"From Sector Four's attack on Fort Douaumont," answered Marat.

"Ah, yes," said Nivelle. Slowly he read the sickening numbers. He looked as if he were sipping a glass of fine wine, rolling it around in his mouth, judging its taste.

"Highly satisfactory," he said, nodding and licking his lips. "The attack must have been a success. How much ground gained?"

Marat coughed. "None, sir."

"What's that, Major?" Nivelle's eyebrows arched. "I thought you said 'none.'"

"I did, sir," Marat said, stone-faced. "The attack failed."

Nivelle spoke through clenched teeth. "Tell Colonel Barc to have himself in my office at six A.M. *That will be all, Major.*"

"Yes, sir," Marat said, with a sharp salute. He did a neat about-face, and left the room.

There was a silence followed by the sound of a man clearing his throat. It was Petain.

"How many men did you lose?" Petain asked dryly.

"Obviously not enough," Nivelle said, his tone close to a snarl. "I cannot take the blame for the failures of cowards under me."

Petain abruptly got to his feet and tossed his linen napkin on the tabletop.

"Leaving, Philippe?" Nivelle asked with surprise. "The main course hasn't arrived."

"I've had enough. Somehow I've lost my appetite," General Petain said with disgust.

"I'm expecting you later, General," said Nivelle. "I'd like your contribution."

Petain gave him a withering glance but said nothing.

Nivelle and Mangin exchanged smiles and shrugs as Petain stalked out of the room.

"He simply has no stomach for war," Mangin said, shaking his head.

"And he will never have the taste of triumph," Nivelle declared, as he poured himself a glass of blood-red wine.

Meanwhile Indy was waiting for dinner with his fellow Belgian couriers in the kitchen. They were a rowdy lot, and rowdier than usual after a few glasses of wine. One ate and drank well at General Staff Headquarters.

The cook, Jean-Marc, was red-faced himself as he prepared a giant pot of soup. He chopped vegetables and meat while taking swigs from a bottle now almost empty.

Indy watched while Rocco, one of the couriers, tried to grab a piece of soup meat on the counter.

"Don't do that!" the cook thundered.

"Hear that growling?" Rocco said with a grin. "That's the little man in my stomach. He's complaining. Not enough food."

"I warned you," the cook snarled, and swung his cleaver. "Your thieving days are over."

Indy watched with horror as the cleaver came down on Rocco's fingers. The man gave a hideous scream. Blood sprayed everywhere. Sobbing, Rocco turned to Indy and held up his bloody, fingerless hand.

Indy turned white, then began to turn green.

And everyone burst into peals of laughter.

Rocco unclenched his hand to reveal that he still had his fingers.

"But . . . the blood . . . the fingers," Indy gasped.

"Tomato sauce," the cook said, smiling.

"And carrots," said another courier, Claude, holding up carrot sticks.

"An initiation," explained Rocco. "We do it to all newcomers."

"Helps them get used to Verdun," said Claude.

"But I guess you don't need it," said a third

courier, Alex. "You got to the front right away."

"Not so nice, huh, kid?" Claude said with a grimace.

"I was in Flanders, but . . ." Indy let his voice trail off.

"But not like Verdun, eh?" Rocco said. "This is as bad as it gets."

"It's an ugly war," Alex declared.

" 'Ugly' isn't the word for it," Indy said. "Truth is, I can't figure out what this war is about."

"Nobody knows what it's about," Alex said, and Claude nodded.

But Rocco disagreed, "It's simple—the Germans invaded Belgium, our homeland."

"So they could invade France, my homeland," Jean-Marc, the cook, added.

"What about Russia?" wondered Claude. "They're on our side."

"And England," added Alex. "They're with us, too."

"Wait a second. I'll explain," said Jean-Marc with authority. He threw two loaves of bread on the table. "This is France on the left and Russia on the right." He put a piece of meat between them. "This is Germany and Austria." He put a waffle above France. "This is Belgium." He put a mug of beer off the coast of

France. "This is England." He put a salt shaker below Austria. "This is Serbia."

"Wait a minute," Claude said. "That doesn't look like Europe."

"What does it look like?" Rocco asked.

Claude looked at the table and declared, "Some bread, some meat, a waffle, a mug of beer, and a—"

"Shut up," the cook said, giving him a rap on the head with a soup ladle. "Now, to continue: when the archduke of Austria is assassinated by a Serbian, Austria wants to make Serbia pay for it."

"What about Germany?" Rocco demanded.

Jean-Marc nodded. "Aha, Germany. They are Austria's friend, and back Austria up. Then Russia, the ally of Serbia, goes crazy and tells Austria to lay off."

"Wait a minute," Indy said, scratching his head. "We're fighting in *France.*"

"Indeed we are," the cook agreed. "France is Russia's friend, and they both declare war on Austria and Germany to protect Serbia. Germany then attacks France and Russia. Next thing you know, England declares war on Germany when Germany invades *their* friend—neutral Belgium—to get at France."

By now everyone was scratching his head.

Finally Indy said, "We're fighting to protect a tiny country that no one's ever heard of. That's what all this is about?"

There was a dead silence.

"I don't know, my friend," the cook said sadly, and went back to stirring the soup.

Indy stood up from the table.

"But the soup is almost ready," the cook said.

"Somehow I've lost my appetite," said Indy.

Chapter 5

Indy went back to the quarters he shared with the other couriers. They were in the former servants' quarters of the chateau that housed the General Staff. He sat on his bunk and pulled out a notebook from under his pillow. He had started keeping a diary. Partly to record all the things he was seeing. But mostly to make some kind of sense of them. Especially when they seemed to make no sense at all—like now.

"I'm at a place called Verdun," he wrote.

"There's a big battle going on here. But it's hard to describe it without making it sound completely nutty. The two armies are both dug into trenches. Every now and then one side attacks the other. The way they do this is to have their men charge machine guns over open ground and through barbed wire. The generals keep saying that artillery will knock out most of the machine guns and that the men's courage will do the rest. *But it just doesn't happen.* The attacks fail again and again and again. The men are slaughtered again and again and again—like animals. And I can't understand *why.*"

If Indy had been able to hear the generals talking at that very moment, he would have had a better idea why the slaughter kept going on.

It wouldn't have made him like it any better, though.

No more than General Petain did.

Petain's mouth curled as he heard General Nivelle complain, "All my officers give me is excuses. Excuses. Excuses. 'The day of the attack was too cold.' 'It was too hot.' 'It was foggy and we couldn't see.' 'It was clear and the sun got in our eyes.' 'We had to charge uphill.' 'We had to charge downhill.' Excuses."

"Excuses for what, General?" Petain demanded.

"Cowardice," Nivelle declared angrily.

"Cowardice?" Petain said. "Do you really think so?"

"I don't *think* so—I *know* so," Nivelle responded.

"And the four hundred and eighty who died today—were they cowards?" Petain asked.

"No," Nivelle acknowledged. "They did their duty."

"Dying—to gain nothing," Petain persisted. "Was that their duty?"

Nivelle shrugged. "It is every soldier's duty to die when ordered to do so. A soldier afraid of death is not worthy of life."

Petain had to pause to get control of his temper. Then he said coldly, "Thank you for that bit of wisdom, General Nivelle. I must put it in the next edition of the infantryman's manual. It is certain to inspire the troops."

"I don't like your tone, General," Nivelle said stiffly.

"Nor do I," General Mangin added.

"Sorry if I gave offense," Petain said sarcastically.

"Death is what war is all about," Nivelle de-

43

clared. "It's the very lifeblood of war."

On that note of philosophy, Nivelle strode over to the map to begin planning the next great attack.

Back on his bunk, Indy still felt rotten. Writing it all down hadn't made things look clearer. Everything seemed even crazier when put down in black and white.

If only he could *do* something.

Then he remembered the one thing he could do. The one thing he *had* to do—find his pal Remy.

Indy had already decided that that was what this war came down to in the end. For the ones doing the fighting, anyway. It came down to buddies sticking together. Trying to help one another survive.

He blew out his candle and tried to sleep. But as tired as he was, sleep evaded him.

The next morning Indy went to the sergeant in charge of his unit. "Okay if I take the afternoon off, Sarge?" he asked. "I just finished a trip to the front."

"Sure, take off," the sergeant said. "You've earned your pay for the day."

The next stop for Indy was the field hospital.

It had been a church before the war and was only five miles down the road. He made it in ten minutes on his motorcycle.

There was a chance he'd find Remy there, though he wasn't sure he really wanted to.

There were two kinds of cases kept in the field hospital rather than being sent farther back behind the lines for treatment.

One kind was soldiers so badly wounded that being moved would kill them.

The other kind was soldiers who could soon be sent back to the fighting front.

"Remy Baudouin?" a clerk at the hospital said. He consulted a list. "Yes, he's here. Ward Eight. Down the hall on the left, and third corridor to the right."

Indy tried not to feel scared as he headed down the corridor. The hallway itself had beds in it, filled with groaning soldiers. Harried, hurried nurses did the best they could to answer the cries and moans that echoed everywhere.

Indy reached a door marked with a crudely lettered cardboard sign. Ward Eight.

He swung the door open and heard a piercing scream. A nurse was trying to hold a patient down.

Two orderlies came rushing past Indy to help her.

Before they reached the bed, the patient managed to get one hand free. He started ripping at a bandage on his stomach.

"Stop it!" the nurse commanded.

"They didn't get it out!" he screamed as the orderlies held him down. "It's still in there!"

Indy froze. He knew the voice. It was Remy's.

"*It is not still in there,*" the nurse told Remy.

"I can *feel* it," Remy cried. "They have to operate again."

"Private, control yourself," the nurse commanded, and slapped his face—hard.

"No! No! No!" screamed Remy as the orderlies began to tie his hands to the bed.

Indy could take it no longer.

"Tell them to stop," he begged the nurse.

"He's a danger to himself and others," the nurse said firmly.

"No he isn't," Indy said. "Let me talk to him. I'm his best friend. He'll listen to me."

The nurse bit her lip. "All right," she said doubtfully. "Other patients need me. You have five minutes."

She and the orderlies moved down the line of beds in the ward.

When they were out of earshot, Indy bent over Remy and said, "How are you, Remy?"

"Could be better, my friend," Remy said.

"I've got a surprise," Indy said.

"Yes?" said Remy, brightening.

Indy grinned and pulled out a bar of chocolate. "The best," he said. "German."

"How did you get it?" Remy asked, taking it with a shaking hand. He had a hard time getting it to his trembling mouth. Glistening sweat beaded his face.

"From a German prisoner," Indy said, trying not to show what he felt while watching Remy nibble on the chocolate as well as he could. "I traded with him for good French bread."

Then Indy had to ask, "What was that fuss all about? The business about your wound—did the surgeon really goof up?"

"No," Remy admitted. He swallowed the chocolate and licked his pale lips. "He got it out, all right." His left eye started to twitch. "But if I get well, they'll send me back to the trenches. So I'm not going to get well. I'm not going back. I'm not going—"

Remy's voice had risen. Indy put his finger to his lips.

"Easy, old buddy," he said. "You read the latest orders? They're shooting any soldier who wounds himself to get out of the trenches."

"*I didn't wound myself,*" Remy said, losing control. "I *fought*. They said *charge* and I *charged*—"

Remy's whole body was trembling. Indy put his hands gently on his pal's shoulders. "Remy, got to get hold of yourself. You have to let your wound heal. Okay?"

"Okay," Remy said weakly.

"I have to go now," Indy said. "But I'll be back. And don't worry, you'll get out of this—somehow."

"Sure," said Remy. He pushed Indy away and turned his face toward the wall.

As Indy walked down the hall, he saw the nurse.

"I'm sorry about your friend, Corporal," she said.

"They won't be sending him back into action, will they?" he asked her.

She looked at a clipboard in her hand, trying to avoid Indy's gaze.

"They *won't*, will they?" he repeated.

"Yes," she said in a resigned voice.

"But he's in no shape to—" Indy protested.

"I know," the nurse said. Her eyes were bleak, her voice tired and sad. "But whenever they get ready to launch a big attack, we get orders to send out every soldier who can walk. There's nothing you can do."

We'll see about that, Indy thought to himself as he headed back to his unit.

Chapter 6

Indy got back to the war faster than he expected to.

His sergeant was waiting for him when he returned to his quarters.

"Tough luck, Corporal," the sergeant said. "Your day off is over. The telephone lines to our artillery are down again. We have to find out how much ammunition they need. Hop on your bike and get the information."

Indy sighed. Back to work. He'd have to worry about Remy later.

He hopped on his bike and headed for the front. He could make good time, at least. Rush hour on the road to Verdun seemed to be over. The road was all his.

The air, though, wasn't.

He heard a buzzing like a fly above him as he raced along the road.

He looked up. He saw a black speck in the sky. Before his eyes, the speck got larger. It became a monstrous two-winged insect. A moment later, it changed again—into a German Fokker biplane fighter.

The black Fokker spat orange fire from twin machine guns. Bullets kicked up dust around Indy's wheels. Indy zigged and zagged his bike. Above him the fighter easily did the same. It was like a giant bird of prey playing with a desperately darting mouse.

There's nowhere to hide, no chance to—Indy thought. Then he spotted a train trestle bridge up the road.

Indy got the last ounce of speed out of his machine as he headed for that shelter. The bike felt as if it was going to shake apart, but it was no match for the Fokker. The plane swooped down and banked in on him, closing in for the kill.

Its twin machine guns blasted away. Bullets came ever closer. Then the German pilot, directly over Indy now, provided the finishing touch for the kill.

A bomb dropped from the plane. Then a whole string of bombs started to fall on the road and the nearby farmhouse. Indy had managed to weave through the massive explosions, until one bomb exploded right in front of the speeding bike.

Indy fought to keep control of the instant skid. No luck. The bike slid out from under him—and he went flying.

He lay face down in the gravel of an enormous crater. He felt like staying there forever. But he heard the zoom of the plane above him as it came in for another pass.

He shook off his grogginess. He forgot about the pain from the cuts on his face. He lurched to his feet and half-ran, half-stumbled to the only thing that mattered—the shelter of the bridge.

He made it—just in time. Machine-gun bullets thudded into the wood above his head.

Peering out, Indy watched the German plane make a slow circle. Then it dipped its wings toward him in a salute and flew off into the deep blue sky.

Indy wondered what kind of guy the German pilot was. Probably not a bad sort. But he'd never know. What a war. You seldom got to see the guy who was out to get you. Machines were taking over the whole business.

Indy walked to his machine. He pulled it upright, got on it, and kick-started the engine. All in a day's work, he thought, in a war where the main job was staying alive.

Indy got a close-up of some other killing machines at the artillery post, when he was waiting for the officer in charge to prepare his ammunition order.

Indy heard a voice coming from a gun emplacement.

"Oh, my Marie, my sweet Marie. You are so beautiful. . . ."

Indy went toward the voice. He stood on tiptoe and peered over a wall of sandbags.

He spied a gunnery sergeant cleaning the barrel of a cannon.

"You'd like a rubdown, wouldn't you, my darling," the sergeant said to the gun, as he reached for an oilcan.

Then he saw Indy.

"What are you doing here?" the sergeant demanded. He gave the courier a hard stare.

"I-I-I heard . . ." Indy stammered.

"Stand at attention," the sergeant barked. "I don't care what you heard. I was just oiling up the trajectory gears. What's your name?"

"Corporal Henri Défense," said Indy.

"Sergeant Jean DeMille," replied the gunner. "From Cannes. You're Belgian, eh? Won't hold it against you. Nice to meet you. You know anything about guns? Every healthy young man loves guns. Come here."

Indy figured he might as well humor the guy. The sergeant must have been shooting off his toys too long. The noise had to do something to the brain.

Besides, corporals *always* humored sergeants. That was what the army was all about.

DeMille pointed to a nearby cannon. "Now what we have here is your basic howitzer. Not a bad little piece of destructive machinery."

"Little?" said Indy.

"It only fires a small shell—like those over there," the gunner said, as he pointed to a towering pile of awesome shells.

"Those are huge," said Indy. He figured each one weighed at least thirty pounds or more.

DeMille shook his head in disgust. "What war have *you* been fighting? You want huge? I'll give you huge."

DeMille led Indy to some truly massive shells, piled on duckboards next to a monstrous gun.

"Wow," said Indy.

The sergeant affectionately patted a glistening gun barrel. "Yep. The Rimailho howitzer. Fires a forty-kilogram shell. Can reduce your average German infantryman to a quivering pile of minced Wiener schnitzel in half a second."

Forty kilograms, thought Indy. That's about one hundred pounds!

"But those are nothing," continued the sergeant, "compared to the . . . big one."

"The *what*?" asked Indy. This conversation was getting loonier and loonier.

"Big Bertha," DeMille said, lowering his voice in reverence.

"Who's Big Bertha?" Indy asked, playing along and whispering, too.

"Not who. What," the sergeant said. "Big Bertha is a Krupp howitzer."

"German?" said Indy.

"What else?" said DeMille, sighing. "It's 150 millimeters of the meanest cannon ever made.

Takes more than a hundred men to load and fire it. Fires over a 900-kilogram shell."

Two thousand pounds? said Indy to himself, gulping in disbelief. This guy had to be crazy. Except that Indy had a strong hunch that he wasn't. No crazier than anything else in this war, anyway.

"Enough TNT to blow this place to the moon," said the sergeant.

"Do the Germans have Big Berthas here?" Indy asked.

"No. Not now, anyway," DeMille said. "But they might. And then . . ." He drew a finger across his throat, making a cracking sound.

Indy's own throat felt dry. He remembered the attack he had witnessed. He could still see the charging soldiers being blown apart—by ordinary artillery. He didn't want to imagine what this Big Bertha would do.

"Here you go, Corporal!" shouted a voice behind Indy. "The list is ready."

A private handed Indy a dispatch bag.

"This has to reach the supply depot fast," the private said. "I think we're going to need shells in a hurry. A lot of shells."

"Another big attack?" asked Indy.

"You know that's a military secret, Corpo-

56

ral," the private said. "But I don't think we'll be using all those shells for target practice."

Another big attack, Indy thought as he climbed onto his motorcycle. He gunned the engine and thought of Remy.

Remy would be going back to the front lines again. The French army needed all the men it could muster.

But what could he, Indy, do?

What could anyone do in this war?

This war, in which machines were taking over the killing because they could do it so much better than men.

But in which men still did the dying.

Chapter 7

That evening Major Marat from General Staff Headquarters, Colonel Barc, commander at the front, and Lieutenant Gaston, from the Sector Four trenches, met in a crowded French café. Most of the other customers were fellow officers, plus a few civilians who still had business in the Verdun battle zone, and girls who had their pick of dates from the military. No ordinary soldiers were there, however, to drink the good wine and listen to the mellow accordion music. Officers had the best cafés for themselves only. Ordinary soldiers had to make do with what was left.

Marat, Barc, and Gaston weren't there for pleasure only, though. While they sipped wine and devoured steaks and french fries, they had a serious matter to discuss.

"The failure of the attack was not your fault, Colonel," Gaston said. "I don't care what General Nivelle says."

"Careful, Lieutenant," Major Marat warned. "A French officer respects his superiors."

"Don't worry, Gaston," Barc said. "All the general did was scream at me. Demand I do better the next time. And order a new attack, of course. An even bigger one. More guns. More men."

He looked away from Gaston and into his glass of wine. He took a drink, put the glass down, filled it up again, and stared glumly into the blood-red wine again.

"It's disgusting," Barc continued. "The Germans know what we're doing. They have their fingers on the trigger every time we come at them. But we never know what they're doing. We have to stake everything on our men's quickness and courage every time they attack. *Why*?"

Major Marat shrugged. "Their spies are better."

Lieutenant Gaston shook his head. "It is not a question of 'better.' They simply cross no-man's-land at night and listen to us. They speak perfect French, so they understand everything we say."

"So it's simple eavesdropping," Marat said.

"Exactly," Gaston affirmed.

"Then why don't we do the same thing?" Marat demanded.

Gaston shrugged. "I've been trying to recruit men. But it's not easy to find ones who can do the job. Frenchmen are splendid at defending their country. But when it comes to learning foreign languages, most Frenchmen aren't very interested."

"Surely there must be a few," Marat said.

"Believe me, I've been looking—with no luck," Gaston replied.

Marat took a sip of wine. Then he put his glass down, his face brightening. "I know where you might find your man."

"Where?" asked Gaston.

"Among the Belgian couriers," Marat said.

"But they speak French just like us," said Gaston, shaking his head.

"A lot of Belgians speak Flemish," said Marat. "That's pretty close to German. It's worth a try, anyway."

"Nothing to lose—except our dessert," said Colonel Barc, getting up from the table and signaling the pretty waitress for the bill. "And no time to waste. Let's go see those couriers of yours. Maybe we can persuade one of them to volunteer."

"Right," said Gaston, as he and Marat stood up, too. He gave a grimace. "I suppose that means giving another patriotic speech."

"It's the only way," the colonel said. "How else could we get the men to do what they have to do in this war?"

Indy returned to the couriers' bunk room right after Colonel Barc had finished his rousing patriotic pitch and just as he was about to get to the bottom line.

Indy saw Rocco, Claude, Alex, and the others standing at rigid attention, and he stiffened to attention himself.

Colonel Barc gave Indy a quick, annoyed glance, and continued from where he had been interrupted. "As I was about to say, one of you has a chance to cover himself with glory. We have a vital need for a man who speaks German. Do any of you speak German?"

There was a dead silence.

"Do any of you *understand* German?" Lieutenant Gaston demanded.

Another silence.

"What about Flemish?" Marat asked. "Surely some of you must know Flemish."

The silence continued.

At last Indy could stand it no longer. He had to find out what was going on.

Besides, helping the major might be more than interesting. It might be valuable. If he got in good with the brass, he might be able to find out more about the coming attack—and how to keep Remy out of it.

He was clutching at straws, but that was better than nothing.

He stepped forward. "I speak German, sir."

"Corporal Défense, isn't it?" said Gaston.

"Yes, sir," Indy said.

"Be in my office in two hours," Barc said.

"Yes, sir," Indy said.

The officers wheeled and left the room. The men relaxed.

Rocco turned to Indy. "Why did you tell him you speak German?"

Indy shrugged. "Because he asked. And be-cause I do. What's the big deal? They probably just need an interpreter. A cushy job."

"Know what the first rule in the army is?" asked Alex, joining them.

"No. What?" said Indy.

"Never volunteer for anything," said Claude, who had been listening.

"You've got a lot to learn, my young friend," said Rocco, rolling his eyes.

Two hours later, in Colonel Barc's bunker of-fice, Indy had a test to pass before he learned the other test awaiting him.

"Let's hear some of your German, Corporal," Lieutenant Gaston commanded.

Indy gave a sharp salute. *"Obwohl ich ein Korporal der Belgischen Armee bin, fuehle ich mich sehr geehrt den Franzosen zugewiesen zu sein."* Then he translated: "Although I am a corporal in the Belgian army, I am very glad to be assigned to the French."

Gaston nodded. "You weren't boasting. Your German is excellent."

"And the patriotism you expressed is com-mendable," added Colonel Barc. "It is noble for you to volunteer for this. The French army will be indebted to you. Indeed, the entire French people will be indebted to you. You are a credit to your homeland. You are a credit to your parents. They will be proud of you. And your heroic deeds will live forever in the pages of history."

"Are you sure you want to go through with this?" asked Gaston, looking at Indy and thinking how young he seemed. No matter how many young men Gaston sent into danger, he never got used to it.

With the colonel's words ringing in his ears, Indy replied firmly, "Yes, sir!"

Then he added in a slightly softer tone, "I guess so."

And in a still more wavering voice, "What is it you want me to do, anyway?"

General Petain (*left*) protests loudly as Generals Nivelle (*far right*) and Mangin (*center*) announce their plan to recapture Fort Douaumont to Marshal Joffre.

Major Marat (*left*) tells a sergeant to give important orders to the fastest Belgian courier. It turns out to be Indy.

Lieutenant Gaston's shrill whistle signals the soldiers to prepare to charge.

Over the top! French troops scramble out of the trenches and meet heavy German fire.

Help from Indy and another soldier comes too late for this man.

Indy and the other Belgian couriers try to figure out what the war is really about.

The Belgian couriers wait for orders at the gates of the chateau at Souilly.

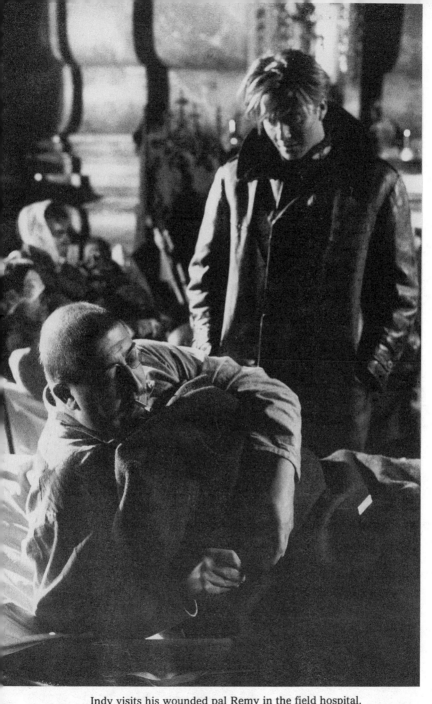
Indy visits his wounded pal Remy in the field hospital.

Indy discovers artillery sergeant Jean DeMille singing to his beloved guns.

Chapter 8

"You look beautiful, Corporal." Sergeant Abu grinned. "Your skin is as pretty as mine now."

The sergeant's skin was deep black. He was from French West Africa, one of the many colonial troops fighting on the front lines for France.

Indy's face and hands were black as well. The sergeant had just finished coloring them with charcoal.

"Glad to see you volunteered," Abu told Indy. "I was getting tired of being the one picked for night patrol. A few words of advice. Never move in a straight line but keep zigzagging. If the German gunners hear you, they still won't have much of a chance of tracking you with their fire. And when German flares go off, hit the ground and hug it. If they spot you, they might take you for a corpse. God knows there are plenty out there."

Lieutenant Gaston arrived to give Indy a final inspection. He nodded at Indy's black clothing and blackened skin.

"Looks like you're ready," Gaston said. "It's a hundred and fifty meters across no-man's-land to the German lines. You've been briefed on the route through our barbed wire and you have wire cutters to get through theirs. When you do, find the command bunker. Listen for anything you can find out. As soon as you pick up anything interesting, or if dawn is near, get back here fast. If you get pinned down on the way back, stay put. We'll hear the fire and try to come to your aid."

"Thanks, sir," Indy said. A hundred and fifty meters meant a hundred and sixty-five yards of bone-chilling danger to Indy.

Gaston coughed. "One thing more you should know."

"What's that, sir?" Indy asked.

"The Germans don't give spies a trial. They shoot them on sight," Gaston informed him.

"Thanks again, sir," said Indy, swallowing hard.

"Good luck, Corporal," Gaston said.

"Luck is what you need, all right," Sergeant Abu agreed, and gave Indy's shoulder a pat.

"Good thing I'm lucky," said Indy, and climbed the ladder out of the trench and into the night.

He *was* lucky in one respect. Clouds covered the moon and stars. The night was as black as his face and clothes. The only light came from random German flares. The only sound came from occasional bursts of machine-gun fire from Germans keeping their trigger fingers limber.

Carefully Indy followed the route that wove through the French barbed wire. The pathway was designed to let the French troops through when going on the attack. The Germans had the same setup. Indy hoped he'd have the chance to find it. Minutes later, Indy was racing through no-man's-land, keeping low.

It was dangerous—but he had to admit it was exciting, too. It was hard not to respond to the challenge of adventure. Out of the blue Indy remembered what an American Civil War general had once said: "It is well that war is so

67

terrible, or we should get too fond of it." What was the guy's name? General Robert E. Lee. Then Indy recalled something another Civil War general, Sherman, had said: "War is hell."

Just then a flare went off above him. Indy dove for the dirt. Lying face down, he heard groaning nearby. It came from a shell crater.

Still lying flat against the ground, Indy wiggled to the crater rim, using his elbows to move himself.

"Help me. Help me," a hoarse voice said in French.

"Hit bad?" Indy whispered.

"Shot in the legs and stomach. Can't walk," the soldier answered.

"How long have you been here?" Indy said.

"Since yesterday," said the soldier. "But I haven't been alone. I had a visitor."

Just then the moon broke through the clouds. The inside of the crater was bathed in ghostly light.

Indy peered over the rim and saw the wounded French soldier lying with his rifle beside him. Facing him was another soldier, a German. Half of the German's face was blown away.

"I took care of him—before he could take care

of me," the French soldier said. There was a funny sound in the man's voice. A cracked sound. "We lay like this all day yesterday. Funny, when he came at me, all I could see was his uniform. But after a while, all I could see was his flesh and blood. Flesh and blood, just like mine. I even looked in his wallet. He had a picture of his wife. She had a baby in her arms. I have a wife, too. And a baby. Why did I kill him? Why did he want to kill me? I want to see my wife again. I want to see my baby. I've never seen him, you know. I was due to go on leave next week. I was going to see him then." The man was babbling, sobbing. "Get me out of here, please. *Please.*"

"I will," Indy said. "I'll get you out of here."

"You're lying," said the man. "You're lying just like everybody else. All I've heard is lies, ever since this war began. The war will be short. We will be in Berlin in two weeks. The war will be glorious. To die for your country is noble and beautiful. Lies, lies, lies. This war isn't fought with bullets. It's fought with lies."

"Honest, I'll help you," Indy said. "Just as soon as I finish my mission here."

"Don't leave me!" The man groaned.

"I'll be back, I promise," Indy said. He tried

not to listen to the man's sobs as he moved out. Sherman was right. War was hell. There was no way Indy would ever like it.

At last Indy made it to the German wire. Working fast, Indy snipped his way through. The night was cool, but he was drenched in sweat. With painful slowness, he crawled along the rim of the German trench. He passed the tops of German helmets. They were close enough to touch. He couldn't make the slightest sound. Once an old Ute chieftain back in Utah had showed him how to silently stalk game. Now he was going after the most dangerous game of all.

He reached a trench bunker, and looked through its slit.

Bingo!

On the walls of the bunker interior hung a full-length portrait of the German emperor, Kaiser Wilhelm II, wearing a military uniform and a spiked helmet, with the tips of his waxed mustache turned up with arrogant pride. Beside it hung a portrait of his wife, Kaiserin Augusta Viktoria, clad in a voluminous white gown, with a diamond tiara glittering in her upswept gray hair, and a necklace of huge, glittering jewels around her pale, plump throat. In front of the portraits two German officers stood staring at a map spread out on a table.

Indy strained to hear what they were saying. But they were only talking about their girlfriends. Totally exhausted, he started to nod. Before long he was snoring so loudly that the German officers heard a faint noise inside their bunker, as if someone was sawing wood in the distance.

They sent a husky blond corporal to find out what was causing the noise. As the German climbed up the rickety ladder leading to the roof of the bunker, the creaking woke Indy. Startled, he sat up and peered into the bunker. The two German officers had changed the subject of their conversation.

"If the French want to attack tomorrow, let them attack," said one. "I don't know whether to applaud their courage or laugh at their stupidity."

Both officers shook their heads, smiling, as they looked at the map.

"So your answer is yes?" the second officer said eagerly.

"Yes, Klaus," said the first one, nodding. "We will introduce the French army to two nice German girls. Our loveliest ones. Both are named Big Bertha."

"Yes, sir," said the second, chuckling the way

officers always chuckled at the jokes of their superiors.

That was all Indy had to hear.

He had to get the news back to the French command—and fast.

Orders for the French attack were already in the works. God help the French army if they were carried out.

Indy thought of Remy in his hospital bed. He would be thrown back into the middle of the bloodbath.

He inched away from the bunker being careful not to make a sound in the darkness. He poked his head up to turn around and wham! His helmet hit the chin of the German corporal, who hadn't seen Indy any better than Indy had seen him! Startled, the German lost his balance and toppled to the ground. But he was on his feet quickly, shooting his pistol into the night and calling for help.

Indy made tracks fast through the German wire. But there was one stop he had to make.

He crawled into the crater where the wounded French soldier lay facing his dead German victim.

"C'mon, let's go," Indy whispered. He grabbed

the man under the shoulders. But something was wrong. The man's arms fell—lifelessly.

Indy looked at the soldier's moonlit face. His lips were frozen in a hideous smile. His eyes bulged open—staring, sightless.

Poor guy, was all Indy let himself think. Time was too short for him to do anything more.

He was just turning to go when a flare went off above his head. In the blaze of light, he saw something right out of a nightmare and screamed in horror.

The "dead" German soldier the Frenchman had killed wasn't dead, after all.

He must have been lying there all the time, playing possum, waiting for the Frenchman to drop his guard.

The guy was a survivor. And now he had turned killer. He lunged at Indy with a fixed bayonet.

Indy scrambled to get out of the way.

Suddenly he felt his feet going out from under him. He had tripped. He was on his back. The German was ready to strike.

Desperately Indy lashed out with his foot. He felt a delicious shock as the tip of his boot hit the German's wrist.

The bayonet flipped out of the German's hand—just as Indy kicked again, catching the German in the shin. Indy grabbed it and turned the point upward.

Now it was the German's turn to fall.

He gave a hideous cry as he hit the ground, and lay there, still.

Gingerly Indy turned him over. The German had fallen on his bayonet. It was buried in the man's chest.

Indy knew he should have felt triumphant. But he didn't. He felt sick.

He had really joined the war now. He had joined the killing. He shook his head. It wasn't for him.

A mortar shell exploding nearby shook him out of his thinking about killing. He had to worry about dying, now.

He crawled out of the hole and started sprinting.

Then another flare went off, right over his head. Machine-gun bullets were kicking up dirt all around his flying feet. Suddenly everything in the world seemed to explode.

Mortar . . . The word flashed in his mind like a spark of light, just before he plunged into blackness.

Chapter 9

The blackness brightened to a ghostly light, though Indy had not opened his eyes. It was as if he were dreaming, but he knew he was not asleep. He only wished he were.

Before him stood a skeleton. A skeleton with wings. Its skull was grinning. Its jawbones seemed to creak like rusty hinges as it said, "Hello, Corporal Défense. Or should I call you Henry Jones, Junior? Or the name you like to go by, Indy Jones?"

"You know my name?" Indy said, trembling.

"I know *everybody's* name," the specter said.

"And your name?" Indy said.

"You know who I am," the figure said.

Indy could not argue.

You could never argue with Monsieur Death.

"I have come for you," Death said, still grinning. "I come for you all, eventually. That is what is so funny about war. The generals on both sides think they can win. But the only one who wins in a war is—me."

He reached his bony fingers toward Indy.

"Come now, my boy, we have a long journey ahead of us," he said.

Indy felt his hand move toward Death's. It seemed to move of its own accord.

With a mighty effort, Indy jerked it back. *"No!"* he said.

"Why fight for your little life? You are bound to lose it sooner or later," Death argued, in a voice as smooth and soothing as syrup. "Come with me now, and spare yourself all the silly struggle, the useless pain."

"No!" Indy said. "I have a job to do."

Death shook its skull. "Don't worry about your job. Your working days are over. I offer you a permanent vacation."

"But if I don't do it, no one will," Indy declared.

"And what difference will it make?" Death asked with a smiling shrug.

"Colonel Barc won't learn about the Big Berthas," Indy said. "There'll be no way he can stop the generals from planning another crazy attack."

"And what do you care about whether the French attack or not?" Death said, mockingly. "Do you really care who wins or loses? Which generals will get the promotions and fame?"

"I care about Remy," Indy answered. "He'll be thrown into the cannons' mouths if this attack takes place. I have to save him. I won't let even *you* stop me!"

Death grinned even more horribly. "Many men have told me that. None made good their boasts." Death extended a skeleton hand to close around Indy's wrist like a vise. "It is time for you to come with me."

"No, I tell you, *no!*" screamed Indy, struggling to break that deadly hold.

"Shut your mouth—or you'll get us both killed," said a harsh whisper.

Indy opened his eyes.

Lieutenant Gaston's face stared down at his. Gaston's hand was around his wrist, trying to pull him to his feet.

"Calm down, Corporal," Gaston commanded. "Tell me, are you in shape to make a run for it?"

"I—I think so," said Indy. He touched his legs, his body. Nothing seemed hurt. "I was just shaken up, that's all." He shuddered. "Real shaken up." He gave his muscles a flex. "But I'm okay now."

"Good. Let's make a dash for it," Gaston said. And they did.

Ten minutes later, they were sipping coffee in Gaston's bunker headquarters. It was terrible coffee. It tasted wonderful.

"I saw the shell land near you," Gaston said. "I figured I might as well go out and see if you still were in one piece. After all, I got you into it. I owed it to you to try and get you out."

"Thanks, sir," said Indy. "I guess all officers aren't—" He stopped himself when he saw the warning glint in Gaston's eyes.

"Remember, Corporal, disrespect to your superiors is a serious offense," Gaston said. "Enemy gunfire isn't the only danger to a soldier in this war. You have to know the rules on your own side."

"Yes, sir," Indy said, biting his lip.

"But let's get down to business," Gaston said brusquely. "Did you find out anything?"

"Yes, sir," said Indy. "The Germans expect a French attack tomorrow. They're bringing up two Big Berthas to blow us to pieces."

"Are you sure of what you heard?" Gaston pressed him.

"Yes, sir," Indy said.

"Colonel Barc has to hear this immediately—while there is still time," Gaston said.

"Still time, sir?" Indy said, playing dumb.

"All signs point to a big attack coming up, the biggest one yet," Gaston said grimly. "Front-line officers like me aren't supposed to know about it, but we do. The troops aren't supposed to know about it, but they can smell it, too. And now we know the Germans know it and have the weapons to turn it into a gigantic trap for us. We have to get that news to the General Staff. Even they won't send us to certain slaughter. They might not mind spilling blood—but they want the fruits of victory."

"But why do we have to go to the colonel first?" asked Indy.

"You still haven't figured out how the army works, Corporal," Gaston said, shaking his head. "It's called the chain of command. A corporal can talk only to a lieutenant. A lieutenant can only make contact as high as a colonel. A colonel can make it to the generals, if he's brave enough—and Colonel Barc is. Understand now?"

"Yes, sir," Indy said.

"Let's move it," Gaston said. He smiled. "Let's see what kind of runner you are."

They raced through the communication trench that led back to Colonel Barc's headquarters. Indy ran as fast as he could. But he found himself trailing the lieutenant by ten yards at the end.

"Sorry, sir," Indy said, gasping for breath, as he caught up with Gaston who was waiting for him. "Guess I got out of shape, using the bike so much."

Gaston grinned. "You're in good shape, Corporal. I was slated to race for France in the next Olympics—the one that the war stopped from happening."

"Maybe you can run in the one after the war," Indy suggested.

Gaston started to say something, then stopped.

"Sure," he said shortly. Then he said, "Let's get to the colonel."

Like Gaston, Colonel Barc was still awake. Like Gaston, he wanted to make sure of what Indy had to say.

"Let's go over it one more time," he said. *"Are you absolutely sure of what you heard?"*

"Yes, sir," Indy said.

"Big Berthas?" Barc demanded. "You're positive that you understood their German correctly?"

"Yes, sir," Indy said.

"And you're sure they weren't making some kind of joke?" the colonel pressed further.

"It's no joke, sir," Indy said firmly. And he repeated word for word what he had heard.

"No, it's no joke," the colonel agreed. He looked at his watch. "Get yourself a couple of hours' sleep, Corporal. We'll leave for General Staff Headquarters first thing in the morning."

"But, sir, I can do without the sleep," Indy said. "Can't we go right away?"

Barc sighed wearily. "You can do without your sleep," he said. "Lieutenant Gaston can do without his sleep. *I* can do without my sleep. But the generals cannot do without *their* sleep. They'll even be annoyed at our interrupting their breakfast—supposing they actually let us do that."

"Yes, sir," said Indy glumly.

"Don't worry, we should still have enough time," the colonel said, putting his hand briefly on Indy's shoulder. Then he asked, "Can you handle a motorcycle with a sidecar attached?"

"Yes, sir," Indy said, brightening.

"Then we'll see how fast you can drive one, at the crack of dawn," the colonel said.

"Yes, *sir*," said Indy.

Chapter 10

The sun rose, clearing the horizon in a cloud-less sky. Its light spread over the gun emplace-ments of Fort Douaumont. Over the cratered no-man's-land. Over the French trenches. Over the old city of Verdun. Over the road that led from Verdun to the French General Staff Headquar-ters in the magnificent chateau in the splendid forest near Souilly.

Young Indy Jones was on a motorcycle tear-ing down that road. In the sidecar beside him sat Colonel Barc.

Indy saw the beautiful brightening blue sky above him. What a perfect day to play ball, he thought. Or go for a swim. Or do just about anything.

Anything, except to go into battle. It was the worst possible kind of day to do that. Bright and clear. The charging French troops would show up sharply in German machine-gun sights. The wounded would broil lying in no-man's-land under the blazing sun.

But that hadn't stopped the French command.

The road was crowded with troops, trucks, horses, mobile guns—all heading toward the front. Indy drove in the opposite direction, through the haze of dust from the marching feet, prancing hooves, rolling wheels.

Suddenly he had to skid his bike to a halt. The road ahead was blocked.

"I'll jump off and go see what's the matter, sir," he told Colonel Barc.

"Good idea," Barc said. "And whatever it is, tell them to clear a path for us. Use my authority. Tell them I say our mission has the highest priority. All their lives depend on it."

"Yes, sir," Indy said.

He got off the bike and headed toward the heart of the traffic jam. He elbowed his way through the men who were slowly moving around whatever was blocking the road. Finally he could see what it was. An overloaded truck had overturned. Cannon shells were scattered over the road. Soldiers were picking them up carefully, while others were righting the truck.

Indy spotted the officer in charge, a captain who was bellowing at his men to speed things up.

Indy gave him a sharp salute and said, "Colonel Barc respectfully asks how long the delay will be. It is urgent that we get to Souilly as soon as possible. The colonel begs to inform you that we have the highest priority, sir."

"Tell the colonel that my orders from the General Staff give troop movements highest priority. But tell the colonel not to worry. The road will be cleared as soon as humanly possible," the captain said. "Five minutes, perhaps—if I can get these men to move. They haven't had much sleep lately." He turned to the sweating men at work and shouted, "This is no tea party, soldiers. Move it! You've got a date you don't want to be late for."

Indy turned to head back to the colonel. Then he froze.

He recognized one of the soldiers picking up shells.

He ran to him.

"Remy," he said.

Remy didn't look up. He stayed bent over the big shell he was picking up. "Act like you're helping me," he said, without moving his lips. "We can talk as we work."

We're like convicts in a prison yard, trying to trick the guards, Indy thought, as he followed Remy's instructions. Then he thought, Maybe that's what we are. Prisoners. Prisoners of this war.

"So they said your wound was healed," Indy said to Remy as they hoisted the shell and headed toward the side of the road.

"They didn't bother saying anything about my wound," Remy said. "This morning all they said was that I should put on my uniform and rejoin my unit. And that I shouldn't waste my breath arguing."

Carefully they laid the shell down and went back to pick up another.

"I shouldn't waste my breath," Remy repeated bitterly. He gave a mirthless laugh. "All I should waste is my life."

"Look, it's not as bad as you think," Indy said. "There's a good chance this attack will be called off. Then maybe you can get back to the hospital. And after that, who knows?"

"*I* know," said Remy, as they found another shell and bent to lift it. "Last night I had a dream. I saw this skeleton—a skeleton with wings. You know who that is?"

Indy gulped. "I can guess."

"Monsieur Death," said Remy, as they carried the second shell to the side of the road.

"What did he say?" said Indy.

"Nothing," said Remy. "He didn't have a chance to. He was just opening his mouth when the nurse shook me awake. But I could be sure what he had to say—as soon as the nurse gave me the news."

"You *can't* be sure," Indy said. "You can't give up hope."

Just then a whistle sounded.

The truck had been turned right side up and shoved to the side of the road. The shells had all been picked up.

A sergeant's voice barked, "Men of the second squad, fall in and move out smartly."

Remy stuck out his hand, and Indy shook it. Indy saw that tears were running down Remy's gaunt, hollow-cheeked face.

"So long, old friend," Remy said, picking up his rifle and field pack.

"So long," Indy said, as he watched Remy rejoin the endless marching line of soldiers trudging toward the trenches.

Indy put his hand to his face. To his surprise, he found that his own cheeks were wet. He shook his head. His jaw tightened. He sprinted back to his motorcycle.

"Let's see how fast you can push this machine, Corporal," Colonel Barc said. "We have lost time to make up for."

"Watch me go, sir," Indy said, gunning the motor into life.

When the motorcycle came to a jolting stop in front of General Staff Headquarters, Colonel Barc released his grip on the sidecar's rim. He wiped a mixture of dust and sweat from his face.

The colonel smiled and said, "Good work, Corporal. When the war is over, I suggest you go into racing these machines. I can get rich putting my money on you. I just hope you can talk as well as you drive. I hope you can change

General Nivelle's mind as fast as you take a curve."

"Yes, sir," said Indy. He thought of Remy marching down the road. He thought of Monsieur Death waiting in no-man's-land. He thought of the clock ticking away to zero hour, when the men would go over the top. He felt his heart beating like the ticking of that clock, each beat pounding through his body. "I hope so, too."

Chapter 11

"Tell me your story one more time, Corporal Défense," General Nivelle commanded. His gaze was cold, his voice icy. He didn't like what he had heard from Indy. Especially since General Petain, standing beside him, had heard it, too, along with the rest of the General Staff.

"I got to the German trench and found the command bunker," Indy repeated for the third time since he and Colonel Barc had entered the chateau ballroom. He was standing stiffly and uncomfortably at attention, since Nivelle hadn't told him to stand at ease. "There were two German officers talking. One was saying that they were going to introduce the French army to two lovely German girls today. But 'girls' was just a nickname for guns."

"And *what* did he call these guns?" Nivelle demanded once again.

"Big Berthas," Indy answered.

"Krupp howitzers," General Petain said. "The biggest guns in the German arsenal. Their killer weapons."

"*I* know what Big Berthas are," Nivelle snapped in reply. "That isn't the question. The question is how seriously we should take this crazy story."

Nivelle shot a glance at his aide, General Mangin. Mangin took up pumping Indy where Nivelle had left off.

"How many of these so-called Big Berthas did these so-called German officers say they had?" Mangin asked, with a trace of a sneer.

"The officer who mentioned them said two," Indy answered without hesitation.

"You see, General, an attack is out of the question," Colonel Barc cut in.

Nivelle cut Barc off with a freezing stare. "You're hardly the judge of that, *Colonel*," the general said. "Be quiet."

"Yes, sir," Barc said stiffly.

"I sense something fishy about this whole thing," Nivelle declared. He turned to Indy again. "You're certain of what you heard?"

"Yes, sir," said Indy firmly.

"No exaggeration?" Nivelle pressed him.

"No," said Indy, as his temper began to rise. Quickly he caught himself and said, "I mean, no *sir.*"

"The lad has repeated the same story three times now, Robert," General Petain told Nivelle impatiently. "Why should he lie?"

"I didn't say he lied," Nivelle said. "I asked if he exaggerated."

He turned to Indy again. His voice kept getting more cutting. "Corporal Défense, you're not a Frenchman, am I right?"

"I'm a Belgian, sir," Indy said.

"So you say," Nivelle said, giving Indy a hard, searching look. "And you left Belgium *before* the Germans arrived?"

"Yes, sir," Indy said. "I fought them on the Flanders front."

"So you say," Nivelle repeated. "Then you say

that you *volunteered* for this dangerous mission."

"I was asked to do it, sir," Indy said.

"I recruited him, sir," Colonel Barc said. "Yesterday."

"I'm not talking to you, Colonel," Nivelle said sharply, and went on with his probing of Indy. "You realize what we do with traitors in the French army, Corporal."

"Yes, sir," Indy said, his throat dry.

"We shoot them," said Nivelle, staring into Indy's eyes.

Indy didn't blink. But he had to gulp. "Y-y-yes, sir," he said.

Finally Petain stepped in to stop Nivelle from turning the screws any more.

"This is ridiculous, Robert," Petain said. "It is clear that the lad is telling the truth."

"Is it?" Nivelle said.

"Of course it is," Petain declared. "You have to listen to reason."

"Reason." Nivelle's lips curled in contempt. "I listen to something far better than reason. I go by my instincts. A soldier's instincts." He gave Petain a superior look. "A *fighting* soldier's instincts."

"And what do those *instincts* of yours tell

you?" Petain asked sarcastically.

"The Germans want us to *think* that they brought up all their Big Berthas," Nivelle said. "They deliberately let this *Belgian* through so they could feed him their lies. Otherwise do you imagine he could have actually penetrated the German defenses and come back alive?"

"And why would they go to all that trouble?" Petain demanded.

"To make us think they are going to attack us here," Nivelle said triumphantly. "They want us to weaken our forces farther down the line. Then they will attack us there. I am sure they are already preparing to make their move, massing their men. But we will fool them. It is we who will attack them where they are weakest. Just as I have planned. *Here* and *now*."

"Nonsense," Petain said. "This isn't a theatrical performance. Those German officers weren't staging a comedy for the benefit of our brave young corporal. You simply don't want to call off your precious attack. But against Big Berthas, it won't be an attack. It will be mass suicide. Or should I say mass murder?"

"I don't think it's necessary to discuss the matter further," said Nivelle with a shrug. "I have weighed everything that has been said. My decision is made."

"You don't mean that?" Petain said, aghast.

"Yes, General Petain," Nivelle replied calmly. "I do."

"You're not even going to investigate this further?" Petain said, unbelievingly.

Nivelle smiled at him as at a child. "Big Berthas? Out of the blue? Why would the Germans do it? Why now? I am not going to waste any more time with this fairy tale. Time is too precious. I want Fort Douaumont before the sun sets today."

"You may not have time to check the boy's report, but I do," Petain said, his eyes glaring. "If those guns are there, your order is folly. Criminal folly."

Nivelle shrugged. "You can put that in your report, General Petain."

"General, with all due respect—" Colonel Barc began.

"With all due respect to *you*, Colonel," Nivelle said with iron in his voice, "I am ordering you to the front to prepare for an attack on Fort Douaumont. I am sick of all your whining. What I want from you is results. That will be all."

He turned to his staff. "Let us go back to the breakfast that was so rudely interrupted. I hope the chef has kept the coffee hot and the croissants warm."

He gave a quick glance at where Colonel Barc and Indy still stood at rigid attention.

"That will be all," he repeated.

Indy opened his mouth to say something.

There was nothing he could say.

There was nothing a corporal could ever say to a general.

A common soldier like him was there for one reason and one reason only.

To obey.

To his dying breath.

Chapter 12

"Lunchtime," the cook said to the Belgian couriers, poking his head into the doorway of their quarters. "You're in luck. I snagged a load of steaks. They were going to the front—but hot meals were canceled for today."

"It'll be hot enough without them," said Rocco.

They could hear the artillery. It had begun an hour ago.

French artillery, thought Indy. Not the German. Not the Big Berthas. *They'd* start when the French soldiers went over the top. He wondered what wave Remy would be in. It didn't matter. Two Big Berthas would be enough to take care of them all.

"Come on, Henri," Rocco said to Indy. "Let's chow down. I'm hungry enough for a dozen steaks."

"You eat mine," Indy said, still lying on his bunk. "I don't have any appetite."

Rocco grinned and licked his lips. "Sure thing. Thanks."

Just then the sergeant appeared.

"Rocco," he said. "Get hopping. There's a dispatch pouch to be delivered fast."

"Aw, Sarge," Rocco groaned. "Can't it wait till after lunch?"

"No luck, Rocco," the sergeant said. "You're the name on the duty roster."

Rocco grimaced. Then he brightened. "Hey, Henri, since you're not hungry—"

"Sure, Rocco," Indy said, getting up.

"Thanks a million. Anytime I can do you a favor . . ." Rocco said, giving Indy a friendly slap on the shoulder.

"Right," said Indy. He didn't mind doing some work. It would be better than lying here and hearing the guns and thinking of Remy.

"Where to?" he asked the sergeant.

"You pick up the pouch at the airfield in Zone Seven," the sergeant said. "They'll tell you where to go from there."

The airfield was less than a mile away. It was a hive of activity. Biplanes and triplanes, fighters and reconnaissance craft were taking off and landing. The French were proving themselves masters of this new weapon of warfare. They were wresting command of the skies from the Germans.

Indy didn't have a chance to look at the French planes long. A pilot, still in his leather flight jacket, thrust a dispatch pouch into his hands.

"Photos—important ones," he told Indy. "I barely made it back with them. My plane looks like Swiss cheese. Thank God we were able to develop and print them fast. Get them to Major Marat at the chateau—while there's still time."

Indy knew better than to ask questions. His job was to obey orders. And his intention was to keep his eyes and ears open. The photographs had to have something to do with the upcoming attack. Only that would make the delivery so urgent.

At the chateau, a guard stopped Indy.

"This is as far as you go," he said. "We've

tightened up security—and Major Marat is in with the top brass now."

"But this dispatch has to get to him immediately. Top priority," Indy said.

"Give it to me," the guard said. "I'll take it to him myself."

Indy gave him the pouch. The moment the guard was gone, Indy wheeled his cycle behind the high hedge along the pebbled driveway of the chateau. Then he raced across an open stretch of emerald-green lawn to reach the shrubbery surrounding the building. Keeping out of sight, he made it to the French doors of the ballroom where he had had his interview with the generals that morning.

The day was hot, and the doors had been thrown open to let in fresh air. Inside, the generals were bunched around a table.

Indy was able to peer into the room through the thorny branches and bright red flowers of a huge rosebush. And he was able to hear everything being said.

So much for French security, he thought. It was as bad as the Germans'. Maybe he should take up spying as his trade. It sure seemed like easy work.

"Surely these photos can wait until after

lunch," Indy heard General Nivelle saying. "I've asked our chef to outdo himself. And the champagne is already uncorked."

"To celebrate our upcoming triumph," General Mangin chimed in. "Douaumont is as good as ours."

"I think you should take a good look at these photos—*now*," Petain said. There was no arguing with his tone of voice.

Shrugging, Nivelle and Mangin looked at the photos. More exactly, they looked at the spots that Petain pointed to.

"The pictures are clear," Petain said. "These are Krupp howitzers. Big Berthas. I see two, just as the young Belgian told us. They're both too far behind the German lines for our guns to hit. But easily capable of ripping our attack to shreds."

Nivelle stared at the photos as if hoping they would change before his eyes. His face had gone pale, almost green.

Mangin's face, though, was red—with rage.

"Who took these photographs?" he snarled at Major Marat. "*I* am the only one who can order aerial reconnaissance."

"I . . . uh . . ." Marat stammered.

"*I* ordered the major to have these photos

taken," Petain cut in. "I am the sector commander, General. I, too, can order aerial reconnaissance when I think it necessary. In this case, I thought it necessary. And it seems I was right."

He turned to Nivelle. "Robert, I believe new orders are needed."

Nivelle still looked as if someone had kicked him in the stomach. "New orders?" he choked out.

"To cancel the attack," Petain said.

"But we've already started our bombardment," Nivelle protested.

"Cancel it," Petain repeated coldly.

"But I have orders from Marshal Joffre to attack," Nivelle said weakly.

"With those German guns, our casualties will be ninety percent—with no ground gained. If you let this attack go on, you will be committing murder," Petain said, his eyes boring into Nivelle's.

Nivelle glared back. "*You* do it, then," he spat out. "You call off the attack. Let it be on *your* head."

Petain didn't bother replying. He walked to a desk, scribbled an order on a piece of paper, and handed it to Marat.

"Major," he said, "see that this gets to the front immediately."

Marat's face betrayed no emotion. But his eyes shone with joy. "Yes, sir!" he said, taking the orders, whipping a swift salute, and nearly dashing from the room.

Indy left his post, too. As he made his way back to his cycle, he whistled a tune that British soldiers had made popular: *"Pack up your troubles in your old kit bag and smile, smile, smile . . ."*

He was still whistling when he got back to the couriers' quarters. He went to see if there were any steaks left.

"You're in luck," the cook said. "Rocco didn't get a chance to eat yours. Right in the middle of chow, he had to take a dispatch to the front. Too important to wait until after lunch, Major Marat said." The cook looked at Indy. "What's gotten into you? You look like the cat that ate the canary."

Indy kept grinning. "I just feel good, that's all. A guy can feel good, right?"

The cook shrugged. "Enjoy it while you can."

Indy was wolfing down his meal when Alex came in. He had a sour look.

"Let's have some coffee," he said. "Late night last night. I was going to sack out this afternoon—but it looks like I can forget that. I'm right after Rocco on the duty roster."

Indy looked up from his steak. "What's the worry? Things are real quiet right now."

"As usual, that's not going to last," Alex said, blowing on his coffee to cool it. "I heard on the grapevine that Headquarters has a visitor. The big cheese himself, Marshal Joffre, is here again. Whenever that happens, dispatches start flying like leaves in autumn."

Indy's face clouded. He pushed away his plate.

"What's the matter?" the cook demanded. "Don't like the way I cooked it?"

"It was fine," Indy said. "My eyes were just bigger than my stomach, I guess."

But Indy's mind was somewhere else.

Alex was right: Big brass always meant bad news.

He had to find out what that news was.

Chapter 13

Indy was behind the rosebush again, looking into the ballroom. The people inside were the same, plus one important addition: Marshal Joffre, plump, sleek, and smiling.

Suddenly Marshal Joffre stopped smiling. He turned to General Nivelle. "Our artillery barrage. It's just stopped. Why? Our men don't charge until"—he glanced at his watch—"over an hour from now."

"Uh . . . well . . . that is . . ." Nivelle stammered.

Petain cut in. "I ordered the guns to stop. Because I ordered the attack to be canceled."

Joffre's face had been flushed from wine. Now it turned a deeper red. "You did *what*?"

"I canceled the attack," Petain said calmly.

Joffre wheeled on Nivelle. "*You're* the commander of the Second Army, Robert. Did you agree to this?"

"I . . . I . . . well . . . yes," Nivelle choked out. "But there's a reason."

"A *good* reason," Petain said. He showed Joffre the photos on the table. "Air reconnaissance. They show without a doubt that the Germans have—"

Joffre, still beet-red, cut him off. "I don't care what the Germans have or don't have, Philippe. I ordered Robert to make an attack, and I want that attack."

"But what possible military objective could it have?" said Petain, bewildered.

Joffre had the sarcastic look of a teacher explaining something to a dunce. "There are bigger issues involved than you could possibly understand," he said. "Fort Douaumont is a symbol of national pride. The public was shaken when the enemy captured it. When the public is shaken, the politicians have a problem. And that means that I have a problem. Does that make it clear to you?"

"All too clear, Marshal," said Petain, unable to keep the pain from his voice.

But Joffre wasn't listening. He had turned to Nivelle.

"Are the phone lines open to the front?" he demanded.

"Yes—finally," Nivelle said.

Joffre strode to the phone, picked it up, and barked, "Get me Colonel Barc."

A minute later he said into the phone, "Barc, this is Field Marshal Joffre. Listen carefully. I order you to *resume the attack.*"

Joffre's eyes bulged as he listened to Barc's reply. Then he shouted, "I don't *care* if you are looking at a written order to stop the attack. You have my *personal* order to—"

Joffre looked ready to explode as he heard what Barc had to say. Then he snarled, "All right, you will have your written order. And after this attack, I will have your head."

Joffre slammed down the phone. "Barc informed me that regulations say that he needs a written order to cancel another written order. He was also kind enough to remind me that the regulation was written by me."

"He refused to do anything?" Nivelle said, shocked.

"All he agreed to do is tell a Lieutenant Gaston in the trenches to ready his men for the attack," Joffre said, his voice still rasping with rage. "Only when he gets my written order will he send the men over the top. Well, that will be soon enough."

Joffre furiously scribbled out his order. He handed it to Nivelle. "To the front, fast."

Nivelle handed the orders to Major Marat. "To the front, fast."

Marat gave a stiff salute and hurried out of the room, the order in his hand.

Indy was moving, too, on the double.

Panting, he reached Alex at his duty post before Marat did.

"Hey, Alex," he said. "Want to trade places on the duty roster? I take your place today, and you take mine tomorrow night."

"You're an angel sent from heaven," Alex said. "I'm asleep on my feet." Then he grinned and gave Indy a nudge with his elbow. "Got a heavy date, huh?"

"Yeah," Indy said. "A real heavy date."

Indy was waiting when Marat arrived.

"Get this dispatch to the front, fast," the major snapped. "It is urgent."

"Yes, sir," Indy said, giving Marat his sharpest salute.

Marat watched Indy run to his motorcycle, jump onto it, gun the motor, and roar off at full speed in a cloud of dust. Only then did the major let himself heave a sad sigh before going back to report to Joffre that the mission was accomplished.

On the road to the front, Indy whizzed past the few trucks and troops still moving. All the rest already were at the front.

He slowed to go around the bomb crater where the German plane had almost gotten him. He gave a look at the trestle bridge that had saved him. This war was going to have a lot of memories for him, he thought.

At last he reached what he was looking for— a long straight stretch of open, deserted road. It would have been the perfect place to push his cycle to the limit and see just how fast it could go.

Instead, he slowed down his motorcycle until it came to a dead stop.

Then Indy moved fast. He hopped off. He opened the gas tank. He rolled up the dispatch.

For a moment he paused, looking at the rolled-up piece of paper. He thought of Barc and Gaston, bitterly awaiting the order that would make them send their men to be slaughtered. He thought of Remy, standing in the trenches with his gun in his hand, his gas mask at his side, and no hope in his heart. He thought of all the other men with Remy, all of them as good as dead. He thought of their wives, their children, their parents, their friends.

It took just a moment to think of all that. And to stuff the order into the gas tank, strike a match, and light the paper.

It took a few moments more for the cycle to explode in a ball of fire as Indy dove for his life into a drainage ditch.

When Indy stood up, his uniform was covered with dirt. Blood dripped down his face from a gash above his eye.

It would take him hours to make it back on foot and report that a stray German shell had knocked him out of action. By then it would be too late to start the attack again. For that day, at least, the killing had stopped.

Indy had made a separate peace.

Historical Note

The French eventually did recapture Fort Douaumont, at a tremendous cost in lives. Thus the Battle of Verdun ended with both sides in the same positions as when it had started nearly a year before. The total losses were estimated at 700,000 men, of whom about 375,000 were French.

General Nivelle's leadership in recapturing Douaumont made him a national hero, and won him command of the entire French army. In 1917, he ordered that army to make a frontal attack on the strongest German position, the Hindenburg Line. The result was a disaster, and caused mutiny in the ranks of the troops. The mutiny was suppressed, with a number of protesting soldiers being executed. But the army became a fighting force again only when Petain took over command from Nivelle and promised that such a senseless slaughter would never occur again.

The Great War finally ended on November 11, 1918, after over four years of fighting, and after America entered the war against the Germans. Over 8,500,000 soldiers had been killed and over 21,000,000 injured, not to mention millions of civilian victims of famine and disease.

At the end of the war, the peoples of the world rejoiced. Their leaders had assured them that it was "the war to end all wars."

In September 1939, Germany, led by Adolf Hitler, and seeking revenge for its defeat, invaded Poland. The Great War became World War I as World War II began.

TO FIND OUT MORE . . .

The Trenches: Fighting on the Western Front in World War I by Dorothy and Thomas Hoobler. Published by G. P. Putnam's Sons, 1978. Retells the combat experiences of French, German, and British soldiers who fought during World War I. Photos of the French in the trenches at Verdun.

The First World War by Dr. John Pimlott. Published by Franklin Watts, 1986. This basic overview traces the war from its beginning to its end. Includes chronology, listing of important war personalities with brief biographical notes, photos, and full-color maps.

World War I (America at War series) by Peter Bosco. Published by Facts on File, 1991. Follows the course of the war from 1915 to 1918, and concentrates on the United States' involvement and the effects of the war on America. Photos and strategic maps.

An Album of World War I by Dorothy Hoobler. Published by Franklin Watts, 1976. Examines the causes of the war and its effects on international political power, the progress of the war from 1914 to 1918, and how the conflict was finally resolved. Photos and strategic maps.

The First Book of World War I by Louis L. Snyder. Published by Franklin Watts, 1958. Explores World War I battles on land, at sea, and in the skies. Photos of the fortress surrounding Verdun and of a German howitzer crew.